BONBONS AND BODIES

A BELLE HARBOR COZY MYSTERY (BOOK 8)

SUE HOLLOWELL

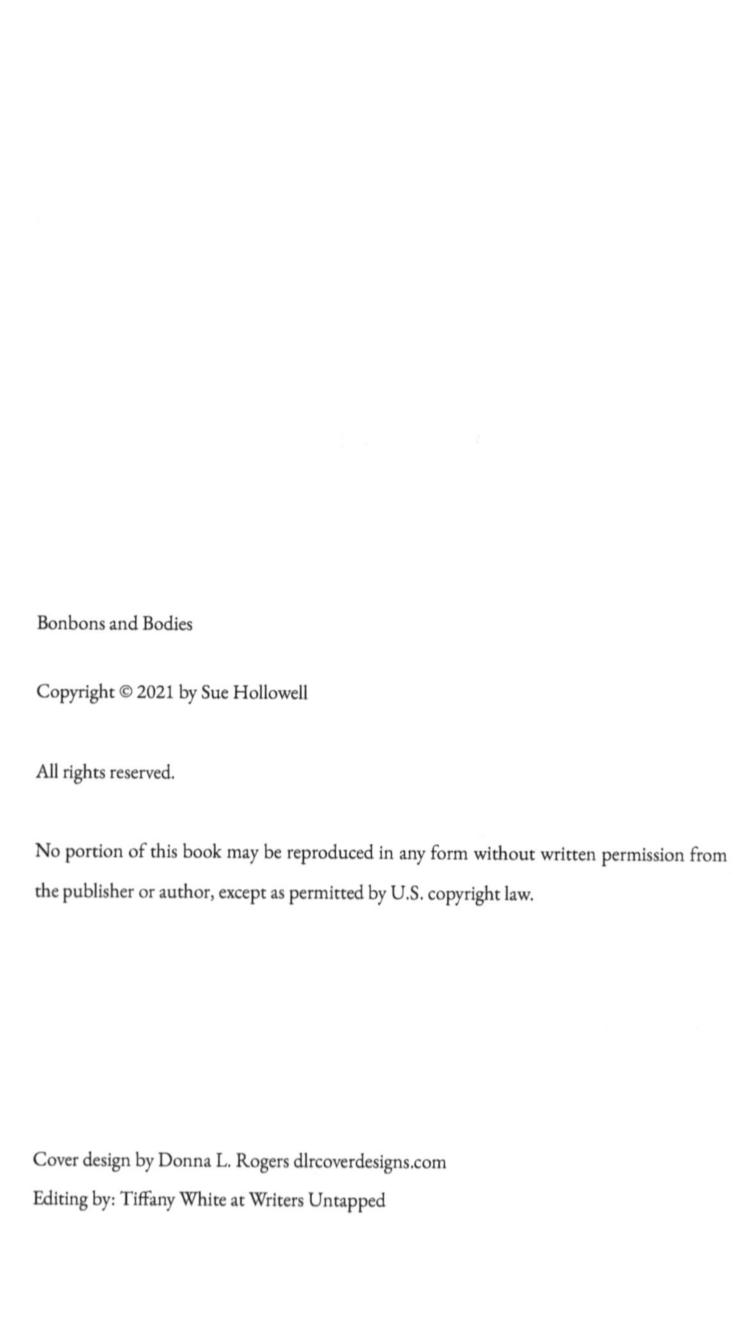

Bonbons and Bodies

Copyright © 2021 by Sue Hollowell

Cover design by Donna L. Rogers dlrcoverdesigns.com
Editing by: Tiffany White at Writers Untapped

Contents

CHAPTER ONE 1

CHAPTER TWO 7

CHAPTER THREE 14

CHAPTER FOUR 20

CHAPTER FIVE 27

CHAPTER SIX 34

CHAPTER SEVEN 41

CHAPTER EIGHT 48

CHAPTER NINE 54

CHAPTER TEN 60

CHAPTER ELEVEN 66

CHAPTER TWELVE 72

CHAPTER THIRTEEN 79

CHAPTER FOURTEEN 85

CHAPTER FIFTEEN 91

What's Next? Sherbet and Shenanigans 97

Sneak Peek of Sherbet and Shenanigans 99

About The Author 103

CHAPTER ONE

The sparse clouds in the night sky reflected the beautiful combination of orange setting sun and bright lights from the baseball stadium. The temperature hovered in the seventies, a perfect setting to watch a ballgame. The seats were packed with raving fans. Food vendors ambled up and down the stairs hawking their wares. Our vantage point was just to the left of home plate, giving us an angle to see the visiting team dugout.

Justin and I had settled into the hard plastic seats for an unofficial date. Unsure of our relationship status, I was open to possibilities. From our recent train trip, and Justin's role in rescuing me from harm, we had grown closer. I looked over at him and smiled. He munched on a big bag of peanuts, decked out in the visiting team's gear, his curly blond hair tucked under a red cap. His muscles flexed with each nut he shelled. He was so easy to be with.

He extended the bag in my direction. "Would you like some?"

Shaking my head, I responded by holding up my box of bonbons. "No thank you," I said. "You?"

Justin tucked his hand inside, removing a chocolate-covered salted-caramel ice cream a little smaller than the size of a golf ball. He turned it over in his hand and popped it into his mouth.

"Mmm," he replied. "Never had one before. Pretty good. And they go well with peanuts."

I was glad that we had this low-key experience together to further explore our relationship. Tentatively allowing my mind to advance in time, I wondered what the future might hold for Justin and me. Was this going somewhere serious? And, more importantly, was that what I wanted? In my new life in Belle Harbor, I was getting better at making decisions from a more deliberate space—taking time to think through and really feel if this was what was right for me. Given that we were taking it slow, I was in a happy place.

Ever since my brother had gotten called up to the big leagues, I vowed I would get to one of his games. For several years he toiled in the minors while working his tail off so when he finally got the call he would be ready. Pacing at first base, pounding his glove, he stared the batter down. Only the top of the second inning and his team was behind by three runs. The pitcher stopped and looked back at the runner on second base, tipping his head down and glaring. Pausing only slightly, he pivoted and delivered the pitch to the batter.

The connection with the ball sent it over the head of the outfielder, prompting his sprint in the opposite direction. The crowd collectively held our breath as the fielder stretched up against the outfield wall and snagged the ball in the webbing of his glove. The runner sped from second to third, diving headfirst into the bag and popping right up to his feet.

My heart pounded. There was a lot of game left, but it would still be a challenge to come out of a hole. At this rate, I might need a few more boxes of bonbons.

The announcer asked everyone to get to their feet as the next batter came to the plate. We stood and cheered as the first two pitches were strikes. One more and we would be out of this mess.

The night sky was now a midnight blue backdrop for the next pitch that was hit high over everyone into the right field stands. Dejected, the visiting crowd dropped into their seats amid a few boos. I knew from attending many games when my brother was in high school that anything could happen. My baseball knowledge was sparse, but until the game was over, they still had a chance.

Leaning to my right, I nudged Justin and pointed to the bullpen. Another two pitchers were up and throwing. Maybe it was for the best. The guy on the mound had allowed several runs and it was early. Some days it seemed you just didn't have what it took and your teammates had to come in to save you.

If it wasn't for my assistant and teammate Linda, I wouldn't be here. Even before I opened Luna's Bakery and Cafe, my little kitchen in the corner of Uncle Jack's antique store kept me so busy there wasn't much opportunity for time away. The pace and success of the bakery required I hire another part-time person to help in the store and with deliveries. I wasn't sure how Dexter was going to work out. He was an eager teenager in need of money who worked his tail off. When I interviewed him I offered free bakery items as a bonus. Without much recent experience with the eating habits of teenage boys, I quickly realized I might have to give him a quota before he ate us out of business.

I pulled my phone from my pocket and checked to see if Linda had texted me. Certain she could handle things and confident she would contact me only as a last resort, I was relieved to see I had no messages. She had insisted I go to the game and no wasn't an option. I worried if she could keep Dexter in check, but she assured me it was all under control. And if needed, Uncle Jack could provide reinforcements.

Standing and raising my arms, I stretched my back and neck. This might be a long night, and I didn't want to wake tomorrow in knots from sitting for hours. David glanced my direction from first base with a brief smile. With his game face on I wanted no part of disrupting his concentration. Playing first base meant you were guaranteed to be part of the action of most every play. He touched the bill of his cap, the signal he began in his early years of playing to acknowledge his family without overtly gesturing to us.

As I plopped into my seat, Justin tapped my knee, touching my empty bonbon box. "Would you like me to get you some more?"

He gestured toward the coach walking to the mound, who pointed one arm toward the bullpen and stretched out the other to take the ball from the pitcher. The bullpen door opened and one of the pitchers who had been warming up trotted from left field toward the coach. Now would be a good time to head to the concession stand, but I decided to wait a bit longer. Shaking my head in response to Justin, I placed my empty box under my seat with a reminder to take it to the trash can later.

The announcer came over the loudspeaker introducing the pitcher who would take over the mound. Just as he arrived to take the ball from the coach, the other pitcher stomped away. After whispering a few words to the new pitcher and pointing toward the batter, the coach put the ball into the pitcher's glove and fell face down into the dirt. Looking around like he had just gotten *Punk'd*, the pitcher knelt down and shook the coach. The infield players and umpiring staff converged on the mound. From inside the team dugout, the doctor sprinted with his medical bag and entered the fray.

CHAPTER TWO

Justin grabbed my hand and we stood. The crowd's silence was only broken by quiet murmurs. Everyone now standing, we waited as the situation unfolded. The doctor waved his arm to bring other medical professionals over. The team slowly migrated to encircle the coach, inching closer. There was no movement whatsoever from the man on the ground. Justin squeezed my hand as we continued fixating on the center of the ballpark, hoping for any sign of life.

David scanned the crowd and made eye contact with me, ever so slighting shaking his head. The crew on the ground remained diligently working on the coach. Over the loudspeaker the announcer asked everyone for their patience. No doubt the game would be postponed. How did that work? Would they start at the beginning of the game? Would they pick it up from where they left off? My mind drifted to the coach's family. How sad for your loved one to head off to work and never make it home. People began to file out of the stadium, apparently concluding the game was over.

"Should we go?" Justin whispered to me.

My eyes were transfixed on the field. Always with more questions than answers, I had to know more about what was going on.

Responding in a whisper, I said, "Not yet."

I scanned the crowd as they swarmed toward the exits. Pulling Justin's hand, I guided him toward the steps leading to the field. We stopped at the railing, almost eye level with the players. They milled about, appearing unsure what was polite protocol in this situation: staying with the coach or providing some modicum of privacy and space to allow the medical team to do their work? Half of the team headed toward the dugout as the rest of them closed in a circle around the coach.

The medics sprinted onto the field with a stretcher. From all indications, there was no hurry. I squeezed my eyes shut, hoping that when I opened them I would see some movement from the now lifeless body on the ground. Justin pulled me closer, our arms linking. I breathed in and out slowly as I opened my eyes.

David's lanky frame ambled over to Justin and me, looking back at the commotion on the mound. I bent over the railing, hugging him tight.

"I'm so sorry," I said.

"It's not looking good," he said, removing his cap and running his hand through his dark, sweaty hair, leaving it standing on end.

"Did he have health problems?" I asked. Not that we all knew each other's business, but maybe David knew something. Certainly in situations like this everyone wanted answers, especially my nosy brain.

David shrugged. "Not that I know of." He turned toward the mound and pounded his glove on his thigh. "And he wasn't that old either." Shaking his head, he continued, pointing a gloved hand toward the coach. "Plus..."

Tipping my head, I waited. There was something he wasn't saying. "What is it, David?" I prompted.

"I'm sure it's nothing. But I saw a giant wad of purple gum laying next to Coach," he said, sniffling.

Pointing to the stairs, I suggested, "Why don't you come sit with us?" I waved him toward me.

Contemplating, he agreed and walked up the few steps to join Justin and me. In unison, we sat in the front row.

"It's just that..." David started.

His mind must have been bouncing all over the place due to the shock.

I reached over and squeezed his hand. "It's OK. Take your time."

Justin leaned over me to look at David. "Do you think maybe he choked on the gum?"

In absence of any real data, speculation abounded to try and fill in the blanks to make some sense of what we saw.

"Unless that was Randy's gum," David suggested.

What was it about the gum that was bothering him so much and why would he be so focused on that?

The loudspeaker barked with instructions for the attendees to hold onto their tickets and pay attention to the media for notice of the rescheduled game. Would people return with the memory of the coach lying lifeless on the mound? How creepy to be the pitcher and have to stand there.

"I just don't know why the purple gum was there," David continued.

I looked at Justin, who shrugged.

"David, what about the gum?" I prodded.

David fiddled with the ties on his glove. "Coach was allergic to the purple. He only chewed the pink. It must have been Randy's," he said.

My stomach tightened. Placing my hand on my belly to calm my nerves, I asked the hard question: "Was there anybody who would want to harm Ernie?"

Whipping his head my direction, David's eyes bulged. "What are you saying, Til?" He glanced at the field and back at me.

"David, it might be nothing. You know how I like to ask questions to understand things," I said.

From my peripheral vision, I could see Justin nod beside me. I needed David calm, because how does somebody just keel over in the middle of a baseball game?

"Well, he was the coach. So of course not everyone agreed with his decisions," David said.

He continued picking at his glove, untying one of the laces and twirling it around his finger. I waited. The stadium had emptied except for a smattering of groups sprinkled around, huddled, pointing and quietly talking. I was pretty sure we weren't going to get answers today.

"I just don't know why he would chew the purple gum," David repeated.

Releasing his hand, I stood. "I'll be right back," I said and scooted past him into the aisle.

When people had a routine, they usually didn't deviate beyond that, especially when it might jeopardize their health. The medical team had hoisted Ernie onto the stretcher with a sheet over him and carried him from the field.

Quickly ascending the stairs to be out of earshot of David, I called Barney. Better be safe than sorry, but he needed to know about the suspicion surrounding the death. If indeed it was an honest mistake, his police investigation would easily conclude. Case closed. If not, we had a whole other can of worms on our hands. One that I really hoped David wasn't tied up with.

Several teammates headed our direction, drawn faces, shaking heads. The shock of something like this, suspicious or not, would devastate people.

"David," one of the guys called. They joined us at the railing, and he continued, "Looks like we'll be here a while. Charlie said not to go far until they know what's going to happen with the games."

David buried his head.

"Hang in there, man. I know you liked Coach Ernie a lot," Randy said. "Not sure why. That guy was a pompous jerk."

Mumbling, David responded, "Yeah, because he chewed your butt so often. But you needed it."

Holding his hands up, the third player stepped forward. "We're all on edge with this. Let's not tear into each other too."

"Joey's right. Sorry, man." David stood and extended his hand to Randy.

Waving him off, Randy replied, "Nah, don't worry about it."

"Since you guys will have some time on your hands, why don't we plan to meet up tomorrow? I can show you some of Belle Harbor," I offered, hoping for some distraction.

The guys looked each other and nodded. "Why not?" David said. "Might take our minds off this." He gestured toward the field. "Thanks sis." Leaning in, David hugged me tight.

CHAPTER THREE

Handing the box of six signature cream-filled cupcakes to the customer, I thanked them for coming to the bakery. We had a brisk pace of selling all day to keep my mind off the events of the night before.

Barney arrived at the ballpark before Justin and I had left. He only had the opportunity to question a few ballplayers that remained and planned to catch up with the others at their hotel before they left town for their next road game. Justin had agreed to stay and allow me to pal around with Barney and stick my nose in his business. Barney had relented as long as I kept my mouth shut. He had figured out by now that my curiosity was unstoppable and had, in fact, benefited his investigations. I had restrained myself from making notes in front of him but tried to commit the key facts to memory for later journaling.

Truthfully, I was also concerned for David's well-being. He was the guy who got along with everyone. And if you didn't like him, he would use his humor to crack through. After a while, you couldn't help but befriend that goofball.

Feeling the whoosh of air enter, I looked toward the door to see David bounding in, apparently no worse for wear from last night. He raised his arm in greeting.

I brushed my hands on my apron and headed around the display counter to hug him. We squeezed each other tight. He held me at arm's length and looked around the place. Two customers remained at one of our small tables, heads bowed toward each other.

"I can tell Mom has been here," David joked.

Playfully whacking him with my towel, I replied, "Yes, that's a whole other story. But I'm thrilled with what she and Dad did to help get this place open." I pointed to a table near the display case. "Have a seat. I'll bring you a surprise."

David sat at one of the white wrought-iron bistro tables, the style a brainchild of my mom. "Not sure if I should be afraid or excited." He chuckled.

Behind the counter, I retrieved one of the cupcakes and plated it, along with a cup of coffee. As I served David, he tilted his head and said, "Is that what I think it is?"

"The one and only," I replied and sat. Linda had things well in hand, and I would get up if another customer arrived.

"Just tell me it's better than those experiments you did when we were kids," David said and dove into the cupcake, inhaling half of it. He pulled it away to reveal cream all over his chin.

"My customers would tell you it is. Those are the bestsellers, here and at the coffee shop where they sell them too," I said.

David gulped down the second half of the cupcake and chased it with the coffee.

I grabbed his plate and returned with two more cupcakes, hoping that sugar high wouldn't keep him up all night. "I should be finished here in a bit and then we can head to Fiona's," I said. "I think you'll really like her."

The only other customers left the cafe, and I headed to their table to clean it. "Let me wrap things up with Linda. It'll be just a few more minutes." I grabbed the empty plates and cups and placed them on a tray.

I joined Linda in the kitchen behind the swinging door and loaded the dishwasher, looking around. She had already prepared most everything for the next day's baking. That woman was efficient.

"Thank you again for closing up. I appreciate it so I can spend some time with David," I said.

Coming around the counter, Linda touched my arm. "Of course. Family first. How is he doing?"

I shrugged. Sometimes his emotions were transparent. Other times he shielded himself with humor. "Hard to tell. But I think he's OK. It will probably hit him when they have to return to the scene of…" I halted, not wanting to finish that sentence. Natural causes were one thing to accept when it came to death, but at the hands of another?

Linda leaned in and pecked my cheek. "Enjoy your time, hon. As you can see, everything is pretty much done for the day."

She gazed around the large kitchen, sweeping her arm in a circle. It was so clean and tidy, you might wonder whether anyone used it at all. That kept us in good standing with the health department inspections.

I snagged my backpack and hooked it over my shoulder, blowing Linda a kiss as I left the kitchen.

David was wandering the lobby and jumped as I said, "Ready?"

Placing his hand on his heart, he nodded. I looped my arm through his as we headed out to the boardwalk. It was another perfect Belle Harbor evening. The temperature still warm enough for short sleeves, the tide calm and gently rushing the shore. The tiki torches lighting our path provided a festive atmosphere. This was one of my favorite times of day to be out and about.

About halfway to Fiona's, David broke the silence. "Really proud of you, sis," he said. We continued our stroll for a while before he said anything else. "For so many things." He pulled my arm tighter through his.

Looking up at him, I said, "Thank you. That means a lot."

"I really admire your bravery to make all of the changes you did to follow your dreams. And it's really paying off too," he said, smiling warmly.

We passed several people out enjoying the ambiance of this little oasis. "Frankly, I'm sure I wouldn't be this far without Uncle Jack. I'm forever grateful for all of his support."

"Yeah, can't wait to see the old coot," he cracked.

The sign for Fiona's bar was now in sight. Per usual at this time a line stretched out the door. One of these days she might just have to expand to include more outdoor seating.

"I think we should invite him and Linda to a game," I tentatively broached the subject.

Stopping on a dime, David looked at me and said, "Tilly, I know some people didn't like Coach Ernie. But do you really think someone would do him in? I mean..."

I tugged to urge him toward Fiona's. "Let's just enjoy our night, huh?" I didn't want to let on yet what I had seen in shadowing Barney's investigation. But, yes David, it looked that way.

Once inside I hoped to divert attention from Ernie's death. Fiona had endless activities for her customers to keep us entertained, and I wanted that detour from the topic, for David's sake.

"If you have time, I'd love to show you more of the town," I offered.

He stopped and looked around, slowing perusing the sights, from the lighthouse restaurant to our right, down to the Ferris wheel on our left at the pier. "I'd love to get to know your world more," he replied.

We stepped to the end of the line to wait our turn to enter. I squeezed his arm. David's phone buzzed.

He looked at it and said, "The guys are already inside. Said Fiona saved us a couple of seats." Holding my hand, he pulled me through the front door as we squeezed past the waiting patrons.

CHAPTER FOUR

e nudged our way through the wall-to-wall bodies. In the distance, the pitcher from the night before stood, about two heads taller than anyone else around him. He unnecessarily raised his hand to guide us that direction. Weaving our way, we emerged into the space next to the two vacant chairs. The giant pitcher high-fived David and hugged him.

Fiona rushed over to us. "We're slammed. So good to see you," she said, staring intently at David.

I looked at David's face, mirroring Fiona. Laughing, I said, "Fiona, this is my brother David. David, Fiona."

They reached arms across the bar and shook hands. Glasses were clinking and silverware hitting plates all around us as the customers enjoyed a later evening meal. David's and Fiona's gazes lingered on each other. I elbowed David, and he swung his head my direction. Most definitely a spark between those two. Pointing to a vacant seat I slid into the chair beside him.

"Fiona," I interrupted her, gazing at David.

She grabbed a couple of beverage napkins and put one in front of each of us. She looked down and shook her head as if trying to gather her wits about her. "OK," she mumbled.

Rescuing my friend, I suggested, "Why don't you get us your signature Paloma cocktail?" From my first visit to Fiona's with Uncle Jack and Barney, her grapefruit and tequila drink had become one of my favorites.

Fiona scooted over to one of her bartenders and placed our order. She glanced back our direction, eyes on David, then me. I smiled big. My friend was smitten with my brother.

Leaning toward me, David said, "Let me do a proper introduction." He gestured to the three guys to my right, starting with the one closest to me. "Randy, Mason, and Joey."

"Nice to meet you," I said. "I'm glad you guys could come out. Fiona knows how to treat customers right."

Right on cue, our drinks arrived. That glistening pink liquid in a tall glass called my name. I drew a long swig through the straw.

"Yeah, we needed a break from the drama," Mason said.

The five of us huddled as close as possible to hear the conversation.

"Can we talk about something else?" David asked, rotating his glass on the napkin, his head bowed. I leaned my head on his shoulder.

Rushing over, Fiona said, "I'll be back in a sec for your food order." Placing two platters of deep-fried ravioli in front of us with a stack of plates, she said, "In the meantime, appetizers on the house."

"Dang. Thanks!" Randy said loudly, grabbing a plate and scooping several raviolis into a pile in front of him. That guy could probably eat both platters and still be hungry for a big dinner. It must take a lot to keep his large frame in tip-top shape as an elite athlete. "David, you should have told us about this well-kept secret."

"Yeah, just recently happened. Right, sis?" David said, his head still perched over his drink.

I elbowed David. "You know. Fiona has hula hoop contests here. Maybe we could do that?" I suggested, trying to snap him out of his funk. But, understandably, the raw emotions of the events shown right on the surface.

The volume of music rose just a hair as several in the crowd migrated toward the dance floor. The boom of the bass bounced us ever so slightly in our seats. If the ambiance of this place didn't perk David up, I wasn't sure what would.

Mason reached for a handful of the steaming squares of ravioli and loaded his plate. I pulled some my direction and transferred several to David's and my plates.

"Look. None of us wanted the guy dead. But you have to admit, he did cause a lot of strife in the clubhouse," Mason said.

There had to be another subject more neutral that we could all discuss. My goal was to distract everyone from Ernie's murder. Not delve into the details even further.

"If you guys have time after this, we can go down to the boardwalk and see some of the sights," I offered, looking between David to my left and the guys to my right.

"Yeah, I'm up for that," Mason replied, tossing a ravioli into the air and gulping it down in one bite.

Everyone processed things in their own time and way. Maybe David just needed a bit more space to reconcile Ernie's death. He seemed to be one of the few that didn't have a bone to pick with the coach.

Raising from his chair, David grabbed his drink and chugged. Was he ready to leave? Whatever he needed, I would follow his lead. My stomach grumbled, reminding me I hadn't satisfied it with enough food. But if David wanted to escape, it would just have to wait.

"Look, you guys," David said, "Ernie was a hard guy to like. But he was just doing his job and trying to get us all to be our best."

David resumed his seat and Fiona magically appeared with another Paloma cocktail. Her smile at David prompted his shoulders to relax a bit. He inhaled a stuttering breath, and I gently placed my hand on his forearm.

"Easy for you to say. That guy never let up," Randy said. "Now, maybe Charlie can step up to be the coach that should have been there all along." Randy pulled the platter of ravioli in front of him and cleared the remaining appetizers.

Holding out my arms in front of me, I interjected, "How about we hiatus talk of Ernie for the rest of the night?" I turned left and right, seeking nods from the guys. Forging ahead, I continued, "Let's order some food, then hit the boardwalk. The night sea air will be therapeutic."

Right on cue, Fiona approached, ready to take our food orders. She placed two more platters of appetizers down, this time, chicken skewers. That girl was generous and incredibly perceptive. I didn't know if she had been eavesdropping on our conversation, but either way her timing was perfect. Each of us indicated our meal choice and Fiona sped over to the server to get those entered in the system.

Returning to us, she removed the empty platters and refilled drinks. Thankfully, she had an incredible staff that allowed her to spend time with customers. She was spoiling us tonight.

Eyeballing me with a grin and a twinkle in her eye, she said, "Did Tilly ever tell you when we went sleuthing out to the farm to solve a murder?" She giggled.

My face warmed. She was not going to rat me out to my brother, was she?

David's head swiveled my direction. "You have a lot going on that I know nothing about," he said. "I'm going to have to visit more often."

Standing in front of David, Fiona regaled the group with the story of our sneaking into a pigpen for clues but only focused on David while speaking. The spark between the two of them was so strong I could almost see the electricity in the air.

David's demeanor continued to relax, thoughts of Ernie sliding to the back for now. I didn't mind being the topic of conversation if it was beneficial to my brother. But Ernie's murder was front and center in my brain. I needed to solve this, if for no other reason than to help David. I shivered as I realized a murderer might be sitting to the right of me, Fiona entertaining all of us in her bar as if nothing was amiss.

Randy had no love lost for the coach. Had he been yelled at one too many times? Did Ernie humiliate him, causing him to snap? I heard baseball pitchers could be temperamental, but many channeled their emotions into their performance. Had Randy's anger gotten the best of him? I leaned away from him and turned my head his direction. He smiled at me. Was that the expression of a killer? And if so, how did he

do it?

CHAPTER FIVE

The bustle of the cafe had kept my mind off of Ernie's murder, mostly. Since our early morning opening, the steady pace of customers had almost bought out our pastries. On most days, Linda and I estimated pretty closely the number of batches to make. But today, we were going to have to do a mid-morning bake, something highly unusual but necessary to keep everyone happy. I could only attribute the extra crowd to the fact that the baseball game had been postponed and people had more time on their hands. And who didn't want to go to the beach?

While Linda furiously prepared several more assortments of goodies in the back, I held down the front at the cash register. Hearing pots and pans clanging behind the closed kitchen door, I tensed. Normally, our process was a two-person job. And even at that, we had our hands full with the variety of goods and the numbers we produced. Our offerings were always fresh the day we sold them, so we arrived uber early to ensure enough time for the volume we had to make. No way would I freeze anything and serve it later. Was it time to hire another part-time baker? Before I knew it, I was going to have to hire a whole crew.

Stepping out from behind the customer in front of me, David raised up. "Surprise!" he said.

Laughing, I said, "Oh, David. You always put me in a good mood." I peered around him to see two others in line. "Why don't I serve the remaining customers, then we can have a quick chat." I gestured to the group behind him.

Turning, he acknowledged them and stepped aside. "That'll give me more time to decide what I want." He placed his arm on top of the glass display case in front of him and bent to study the choices.

"Linda has more coming soon. You can have something right out of the oven, if you can wait a bit," I said to him. "What can I get you?" I asked each of the next two customers who chose the final selections of cupcakes.

David's jaw dropped then clamped shut, as I loaded the remaining cupcakes into to-go boxes, thanking the customers and inviting them to return.

I wiped my hands on my apron and joined David in the lobby, gesturing to a vacant table for a quick chat until either Linda or a customer needed me. "That was a lot of fun at Fiona's last night," I said, hoping he focused on the joy and not the murder.

David looked down, fidgeting with his fingers in his lap.

Reaching across the table and clasping his hand, I said, "I'm very sorry about Ernie. We'll figure this out."

"You mean..." he started, grinning.

Holding up a hand, I said, "Stop right there. What I meant was, I'm sure Barney will figure this out." Barney had previously admonished me for inserting myself into his business. Publicly, it couldn't be known that I was involved. But even though I couldn't afford the time to get caught up in another investigation, I had to do this for my brother. I was busier in my new cafe than a one-armed paperhanger. I barely had time to spend with David, but thankful for Linda—she was pulling double duty to help me out. I owed her big time.

"Plus, I think we should explore Belle Harbor. There's lots of great escapes here." I stood as Linda emerged from the kitchen, holding two trays of cupcakes to load into the display case. Joining her behind the counter, I grabbed a tray and slid several cupcakes onto a shelf and two onto a plate for David.

David joined us at the counter, reaching for the plate. I laid a napkin on top and handed it to him. "I'll trade you the plate for the tray." He chuckled. Although I think he was mostly serious.

"Dude, you're going to eat up all of our profits," I chided, handing the empty tray to Linda. "Thank you so much for those, Linda. I'll try to keep my brother out of the customer supply."

"Hey," David yelped with cream on his face again, reminiscent of Uncle Jack diving into the cupcakes in exactly the same way.

As if customers knew exactly when we replenished our cupcake supply, several appeared in the cafe. Our kitchen oven vented toward the beach, not by design, but it certainly helped attract customers, who followed the sweet smell. The rush immediately depleted about half the batch just loaded into the case.

Joining David in the lobby, I suggested a few sites to explore today. The longer the day went on, the fewer the customers we generally had, most people wanting a morning treat and then lunch. Typically, Linda was able to handle the cafe alone later in the afternoon. Knowing she may not always be available, I made a mental note to begin a search for another new team member. Just Dexter working here a few hours a week wouldn't be enough.

I packed up a couple of the chicken salad wraps in a bag for us to have later during our travels. After loading them and a couple of bottles of water in my backpack, I joined David to map out our plan. We agreed to hit the carousel in the little shopping center first. I was certain I could keep him distracted with the multitude of little stores inside, from toys to hats. Thanking Linda, I grabbed David's hand and we exited the cafe.

The warmth of the afternoon sun hit us like a blanket as we headed toward the boardwalk. I removed my sweater and tied it around my waist. Stopping for a moment, I gazed at the glistening peaks of water as the waves hit the shore. I vowed never to take this for granted just because I lived here. The light breeze waved the palms at the top of the trees. Families still filled the beach at this time of day, squeezing every moment out of their time.

Pointing toward our destination, I led David to our afternoon of amusement.

"So, Fiona," I said, snickering and waiting for David's response.

He didn't bite, keeping his gaze straight ahead.

Not letting him off the hook, I continued, "You two seemed to have a spark." I kept my eyes forward, knowing full well I was making him squirm.

Stoically, he warded off my teasing.

"Maybe we should head back there again for dinner tonight," I suggested. One way or another I would prompt a response.

"Really?" he said excitedly, glancing at me and then quickly focusing back on our destination.

He was easy prey sometimes. I felt a little guilty, given his emotional state with the murder of Ernie. But hey, I was his sister, so I was obligated to the good-natured ribbing. "Yeah, she's pretty awesome. Really glad she and I became friends. She's gotten me out of my shell too," I said, happy to play my part in any matchmaking between my bro and bestie.

I stopped, pointing to the Ferris wheel and looking at David. He shook his head. "Nope."

"So you're OK going in a circle as long as you don't leave the ground," I said. "Got it." I tucked my arm under his elbow as we strolled toward the carousel. I wouldn't wish anyone dead, but thanks to Ernie I was getting quality time with my brother. I didn't realize how much I had missed him. And, truthfully, my parents too. Their visit from Boston was the first time I had seen them since I had escaped my former life and arrived in Belle Harbor.

The nerves I had prior to their arrival could have turned my entire head of hair prematurely gray. I had imagined in my mind all of the conversations we might have when they visited about my failed marriage and their disappointment with my life. Somehow, it turned out to be as far from that judgment as possible. No small thanks to Unkie.

He played interference, mostly with my mom, to ease the introduction of them to my new home. I missed them like crazy and couldn't wait to see them again.

I really did need to figure out how to get more help at the cafe so I could pay them a visit. And perhaps travel a bit more to visit my brother as the team played in different cities.

"You should give me your schedule so I can plan a trip to see you," I said.

His face expanded into the biggest grin. "I would love that," he said as we turned into the shopping center, the carousel rotating with circus music blaring throughout the mall.

CHAPTER SIX

David led the way to the ticket booth and paid for our turn on the carousel. Glancing around, I noticed we were the oldest kids in line for the ride. However, my younger brother appeared unfazed at the disparity in age between him and the other riders. The music slowed a bit as the carousel stopped, allowing for one group to depart and another to join. Choosing a bench instead of a horse, we both climbed in. I had yet to experience this part of Belle Harbor, feeling a bit out of place as an adult. However, I was fully engaged with David's adventurous spirit to explore the shops.

The carousel circled about ten times, slowing to moans of "keep going."

Looking at David, I raised my eyebrows, inquiring whether he wanted to take another spin.

"Maybe later," he said as we departed the ride.

Wobbling down the steps, I bumped into him and clutched his arm, both of us tumbling to the floor. Well, that's some grace for you. He lifted me up, dusting off my shoulder and picking a piece of sticky taffy from my elbow and holding it out to me. He laughed, throwing it into the trash.

"I think we just decided our next stop," he said.

I followed him to Daffy Taffy, where there seemed to be hundreds of flavors to choose from. With the sweets from the bakery, I had all the sugar I could handle. But my curiosity got the best of me as I wound my way through displays of over one hundred and seventy flavors of salt-water taffy. David grabbed a bag from the dispenser and began to load it up with several flavors.

"How can you choose? It's overwhelming," I said, continuing to zombie-walk through the aisles.

David handed me a bag and said, "Just start. Here." He plopped a butter toffee flavor into my bag.

"Nah, this isn't working. I have to be orderly," I said and left David behind.

I was nothing if not organized. Returning to the beginning, I started with flavors beginning with the letter A and grabbed a handful of each of the first ten flavors, ending with black forest cake. Ten flavors at a time would take me at least seventeen visits to try them all. David joined me, holding up his bag, which must have weighed about five pounds. I sincerely hoped he was going to share that with his teammates.

"I'm ready," I said as we headed to checkout.

We fastened our bags and loaded them into my backpack, David taking over carrying it around as we weighed it down.

Strolling around the carousel at the center of the mall, we passed by a toy store. I stopped and glanced at David, and he shook his head. OK, maybe later. We continued on, stopping at each shop, gazing into their display windows. The next one held watercolor seaside paintings. Beautiful renditions of Belle Harbor in all its glory throughout the four seasons.

"You know, I think turnabout is fair play," David said as we continued our leisurely stroll.

I knew darn well where he was going with this, the little stinker, but I wouldn't bite. "We need to stop by Unkie's sometime soon too," I suggested, planning to invite Uncle Jack and Linda to David's game before the team left town.

"Nice try. So Justin," he said.

We stopped just inside the front of the hat store, several silly, whimsical choices in the display window beckoning us to try them on.

Ignoring David's prompt, I grabbed a floppy, teal-colored hat with fuchsia feathers standing up and placed it on my head. "Am I ready for the Kentucky Derby?" I asked, glancing in the mirror.

David reached for a black pirate hat with a white skull and cross-bones on the front and black braids draped down the sides. "Argh, matey," he growled in his best pirate voice. This adventure was most definitely easing the tension for him. Mission accomplished. He returned the hat to the display. "Still waiting for your answer," he prompted. Grabbing a tall, red- and white-striped Dr. Seuss Cat in The Hat, he pulled it down around his ears and shook his head for the hat to jiggle.

Winding our way further into the store, I grabbed a 1920s hat, described as a flapper cloche. The knit crotched cream-colored hat held a large flower on the side with a shining pearl accent. Not something you would likely need in Belle Harbor. Placing it on my head, I glanced in the mirror as it covered most of my short hair.

"All right. Yes, we're something. But I'm not exactly sure what yet. Are you happy?" I softly punched him in the arm.

"Are you happy?" he asked with all seriousness. "That's all I want to know."

David grabbed a fedora companion to my flapper hat and pulled out his phone for a selfie with me.

"Yes. And send me that pic please."

We returned our hats and quietly worked our way to the exit, trying on several more styles. If I stopped for a bit to think, I realized I was very happy. My new life in Belle Harbor had everything I had ever wanted. The cafe was booming. Uncle Jack and Linda were engaged and my closest family. My bestie Fiona was a riot and partner in sleuthing. And Justin. For now, I kept my expectations low. I didn't want to be disappointed, but I was hopeful for the possibilities. We were friends before we started getting more serious, so I knew I really liked him. He was kind, a hard worker, and if I allowed my mind to wander, I honestly could see myself with him for the rest of my life.

My heart fluttered at my thoughts as I realized David was nowhere near me on the outside of the store. Deep in my thoughts, I had wandered away from him. I glanced throughout the mall to find where he had gone. He must still be in the hat store. Maybe he couldn't resist that pirate hat. The guys would get a big kick out of that.

I reentered to find him staring at one of his team's baseball caps in his hands. "David?" I asked. I hoped our adventure wasn't about to abruptly be cut short with a return to the ominous subject of Ernie's murder.

"What?" he asked, snapping out of his trance. "Oh, Tilly. What did you say?" He slowly placed the cap on the display mannequin.

"Let's head out and eat our lunch," I suggested.

He didn't move, shaking his head, clenching his fists. I so wished I could take his pain away. "There's just something not right," he mumbled, continuing to stare at the hat. "I didn't realize it until now." He slowly turned his head toward me, intently staring like he was trying to impart his thoughts.

"What are you talking about?" If he was open to discussing the subject, I was all in for him. Until this was solved it didn't seem like he would have much peace.

He grabbed the hat again and held it out to me, pointing at the bill. "Do you see this emblem where it shows it's official team gear?"

I nodded, no clue where he was going with this.

"Randy's hat at the game the other night didn't have that," he blurted, shaking the hat at me.

Still not following, I replied, "So?"

"So," he said. "Why would he be wearing a non-sanctioned hat?" He shook his head, replacing the hat and heading for the exit. Just outside the door, he turned and said, "Tilly, I really don't want to think Randy had anything to do with Ernie's death." He turned to see who was nearby and stepped closer to me, lowering his voice. "But nobody knew better than I did how much he hated that guy."

I grabbed his arm and pulled him into a nearby hallway. "David, no."

He nodded. "I have to consider it. I mean someone killed Ernie, and Randy had all of the reasons. I just don't know if he had it in him."

Our nice, relaxing outing appeared to be coming to an end.

My stomach grumbled. "Let's sit and eat," I said. Until this was solved, we had to be careful about who we hung out with. The list of suspects was long and growing.

CHAPTER SEVEN

Fiona arrived juggling arms full of take-out food from Tuscany Italian Restaurant. I was hoping for a nice, fun-filled evening as far away from Ernie's murder as possible. My little cottage would barely hold the group, but I wanted safe, familiar territory for David. Leaving him after our jaunt to the carousel mall, my heart was heavy. His coach had been murdered, and one of his best friends was a prime suspect. Barney had been visiting the hotel where the players were staying and interviewing a group at a time. David had yet to have his turn. Would he share what he knew with Barney at the risk of his friend being arrested? The alternative consisted of letting a possible murderer go, and David would not choose that route.

Unpacking the bags of food, Fiona lined up the boxes on the counter facing the kitchen. "Be right back," she said and headed out the front door. That girl was a surprise a minute. No doubt she had something in store for tonight as well. Returning from her car, she entered with another armload of take-out bags. I raced to rescue the food from ending up all over the floor.

"Are you kidding?" I laughed, grabbing several bags and heading to the small, round dining room table. "Did you buy them out?" I counted fourteen bags of food to feed six people. But seeing the guys eat at Fiona's the day before, I estimated she was probably spot on.

"I'm pretty good at sizing up how much people are going to eat," she said as she placed several bags in the kitchen. "I think we can put out a few things and keep the others warm in the oven."

Looking around, I saw all the surfaces were covered in bags from Tuscany. "Is there more in your car?" I asked, heading to close the door.

"That's it from Tuscany. But I do have the fixings for drinks," Fiona said, escaping to retrieve the coolers of beverage ingredients.

Shaking my head, I was continually stunned at Fiona's generosity. "I'm paying for half of this," I offered as she returned.

I arranged the food containers and set out plates and utensils for our guests, bringing some order to the chaos. "I think you're going to need to upsize your bug to a van if you keep up this delivery stuff."

"Yeah, surprising how much that little thing can fit, though." Fiona carried a cooler to the kitchen and began preparing a drink for each of us.

I pulled out a stool from the counter and sat as we took a quick break before our guests arrived. "Cheers," she said as we clinked glasses.

Sipping the sweet liquid, I smiled. I loved every part of my life.

"What?" Fiona asked, fiddling with the boxes to situate them just right.

"So glad we met and became friends," I said, turning the glass on the counter, leaving a wet ring. I wiped the moisture and dried my hand on my shorts.

Fiona chuckled. "The adventure in my life has amped up a bit since I've met you too."

I shook my head. "I can't imagine that."

Fiona pulled out a stool next to me and sat. The clock on the microwave showed we only had a few minutes before everyone was scheduled to arrive. "So catch me up. Have you solved the case of Ernie's murder yet?" she asked, slurping her drink.

I stood, my nerves starting to prickle. "It's weird." Moving into the kitchen, I peered out the window into the night. The next-door chickens quietly went about their business, barely making any noise.

Visions of the previous neighbor, laying on the floor of his entryway, being attacked by those little ladies, made me smile. He deserved that and more for what he had done. Good riddance to him.

"Well, of course it's weird. Somebody's a murderer. That's not normal behavior," Fiona replied.

"So," I said, "Ernie in the center circle of my clue chart. Really only a couple of others, but no strong contender at this point."

"OK," Fiona prompted.

"The most likely person is Randy." I refilled my glass from the pitcher Fiona had prepared. Setting the glass aside, deciding I better pace myself, I grabbed a bottle of water.

"You have to remain neutral. So tell me factually why it might be him."

I needed to visually see this on paper. A picture in front of me always triggered different brain waves to further my analysis. I got a piece of paper and pencil from a kitchen drawer. I placed Ernie's name in the middle and drew a line out to Randy. "Not unusual for sports players, he had conflict with the coach."

"Was it any different than the other player-coach relationships?" Fiona asked.

Looking at her, I tipped my head. "Not sure. But one thing David noticed that might be nothing is that the night of the murder, Randy had on a hat that wasn't part of the uniform. What would he be doing that he lost his cap?"

"I'm with you now. That is weird. Teams are sticklers with uniform compliance."

Pounding on the door and bell ringing interrupted our discussion. Oh, my goofy brother and his friends. Never a dull moment. Shoving the paper into the drawer I went to let them in before they broke through.

"C'mon in guys." I gestured into the room as they entered. In addition to the same crew at Fiona's last night, another person had joined the group. An older gentleman who was obviously not one of the players.

"Til, I hope you don't mind. We brought Charlie along to get him out of the hotel," David introduced.

Charlie held out his hand. "I'm sorry you're his sister," he chided, nodding toward David.

"Hey," David said, putting his arm around the old guy. "But I guess I better be nicer to the coot, as he's now the head coach."

Fiona made eye contact with me. Message received. We knew nothing about Charlie, but we just discovered a motive for his wanting Ernie out of the way. Another circle for my clue chart, and tonight would be a prime opportunity to squeeze the guy for info. Jumping right into bar owner mode, Fiona had already lined up drinks for everyone.

I sidled up to David, giving him a hug. His demeanor had improved from the sullen mood earlier today at the carousel mall. Either he was ignoring reality or possibly accepting it.

"Glad you guys came and brought Charlie too," I said. David didn't need to know about my clue chart in the drawer and my mission to further flesh it out from tonight's festivities.

"Thanks for inviting us. Sometimes these goons can be unruly," David said.

I pulled him into a corner in the kitchen as far away from the group as possible. Fiona seemed to always have snooping on her mind and tonight was no different. Before the guys had arrived, she suggested herself, David, Justin, and I return to the scene of the crime late tomorrow night. While I agreed it could enlighten our path to the truth, I was already conjuring up excuses to use if we got caught. We could maybe explain that David needed his medication and he forgot it in his locker. I only hoped we wouldn't find ourselves in the slammer, which was a very real possibility.

The remainder of the night, I forced my mind to focus on being present with my brother, to enjoy this opportunity I had for an extended visit with him. Tomorrow would be soon enough to pick up the investigation.

CHAPTER EIGHT

Fiona's getaway vehicle barely fit the four of us, but she was the only one with a car. Instinctively she parked in the corner of the parking lot near a clump of trees and as far away from the entrance to the stadium as possible. We awkwardly piled out and quietly stood, Fiona with her index finger on her lips to signal silence. The sun had been down a couple of hours, but the night sky was relatively free from clouds and lit by stars and half a moon. Reaching into her backpack, Fiona retrieved flashlights for each of us. I wondered what other sleuthing tools she had stuffed in there.

We huddled next to each other as Fiona suggested a strategy. David nodded, acknowledging her plan. First, we would start at the perimeter and methodically work our way to our destination, the pitching mound, where Ernie took his dive. We had a lot of ground to cover.

Thankfully, with four of us we'd have plenty of coverage to remember details I could note in my sleuthing chart.

I inhaled deeply as we began our trek to enter. Justin grabbed my hand and squeezed, smiling huge. He was enjoying this. I just hoped between him and Fiona, this didn't become a regular routine.

The front of the stadium had giant baseball caps to each side of the entrance. They were raised on pillars above the ground as a canopy to shade the incoming crowd from the sun. Heading to the front door, Fiona jiggled the handle. I guess start simple to see if something was unlocked. No dice. She and David tipped their heads together, whispering. David pointed toward his right, indicating another possible entrance. We had yet to need our flashlights. Stealthily, we wound our way around the stadium to a door labeled *Maintenance*. David tried the handle, and sure enough, it opened.

If I had any doubts about proceeding, they flew out the window. We were about to travel beyond a point of no return.

David waved us inside the dark hallway. Behind me, Justin slowly closed the door with a click. We held our ground for several seconds, listening. Fiona switched on her flashlight, which was sufficient for all of us to see the path ahead.

As we clustered together, David whispered, "The guards normally make rounds every hour. First the edge, then the inside. If we're lucky, we can just follow his sequence."

How could he possibly know that? Most definitely a question for a later time. Assuming we got out of this unscathed.

We fell in line behind David, who led us from the hallway to the ground level walkway that encircled the play field. Without knowing exactly what we were looking for, we had to cover everything. We emerged into an area that normally would have been packed with game attendees standing in line for food or souvenirs. All the stations had rolling metal doors that were closed. The night sky and the security lights scattered throughout were sufficient to illuminate our route. Nothing in this area looked even close to providing a clue.

A considerable clang of metal sounded behind us, causing everyone to jump in unison. How would I ever make it out of here with my sanity intact? Placing my hand on my heart to slow my breathing, I followed David and Fiona as they resumed our quest. Without incident or discovery of any new clues, we wound our way through the entire lower-level concourse, returning to where we had entered.

Looking both ways, David whispered, "I think we should head to the lockers next."

Now you're talking.

"I saw the guard just coming out of there," he continued. "From there, we can get to the dugout."

David guided the four of us about twenty yards back from the direction we had just come and turned down another hallway. He flipped his light on low as we passed several doors until we arrived at the one labeled *Locker Room*. Expecting this might be the end of the road, I was pleasantly surprised the door was unlocked. Following him, we continued further into the bowels of the stadium. The smell of dirt, stale sweat, and for some reason coffee permeated the air. Perhaps we were near the guard office where someone brewed a fresh pot to make their rounds.

I couldn't let my mind go through all of the possibilities were we to get caught. Would we do jail time for trespassing? Get busted for trying to steal something? Trusting David, we entered the room with lockers bordering three walls with benches in front of each set. Offices lined the fourth wall with a hallway between two of them that looked like it led toward the field. We needed to spend a chunk of time here to thoroughly evaluate any possible clues.

Sitting on the bench closest to me, I panned the room, envisioning it filled with players, coaches, and supporting personnel getting prepared for the game. Would the coaches be in the office just before game time? Would they be out with the players in the locker room? Or elsewhere?

Fiona sat next to me as David and Justin stood to our side. I really hoped the guard was far enough away so he couldn't hear our talking because I had to quiz David. There was only so much one could obtain just by surveillance.

Beckoning David as close as possible, I asked, "Can you tell us about the game-time routine? Especially where the coaches would be?"

He circled the locker room, returning to my side, and said, "They're in the offices to start off." He straightened and looked around. "Then, they normally head out to the field to oversee warm-ups."

I stood. "Would they come back in here after that?" I wasn't going anywhere with my line of thinking, only gathering details that I hoped would lead me in a solid direction.

David shrugged. "Sometimes. I really don't pay a lot of attention. I'm in my own pre-game routine." Strolling away, he mumbled, "Maybe I should have."

"Can you show us your locker?" I asked. Maybe resuming that vantage point could trigger a memory for him.

Leading us to the row of lockers on our left, he stopped mid-way and pointed. His jersey with number twenty-four was on a hangar with Griffin lettered on the back, cleats on the bottom shelf next to his glove. Just to the right was Randy's locker. I stepped to the side and studied its contents, identical to David's, except for two pouches of purple gum. Without alerting David to my observation, I noted that critical fact. Perhaps it meant nothing. But the coach's severe allergy to that flavor of gum must have been somewhat known by the players. Was Randy careless somehow? Could that explain why the coach had the purple gum? Or with full knowledge, did Randy replace the coach's gum with one he knew might kill him?

CHAPTER NINE

Gazing into Randy's locker, David shook his head. Was he finally coming to the realization that Randy may have been involved? Perhaps Randy had teamed up with another person to contaminate the gum. Silently we all filed around the perimeter of the room, glancing in each locker. Without a word, David switched his flashlight on low and guided us down the hallway toward the dugout. I closed my eyes for a second to imprint the contents of the locker room in my brain.

Justin squeezed my hand, leaned in, and whispered, "Let's go."

I nodded, and we resumed our exploration of the vacant stadium. I felt in my gut we were getting closer to knowing details that could paint a picture of what happened to Ernie just a few nights ago. The only sound was our sneakers on the concrete and the moans and groans of a giant old building. In the distance, I could hear cars passing by on the road but nothing nearby. So far, we had escaped detection by the guard. We needed to continue our pace to keep ahead of his rounds. Did David know the guard? If so, perhaps if we did get caught we could talk our way out of it. While we were sleuthing for clues to Ernie's murder, my brain needed to find that excuse.

We silently emerged from the hallway into the dugout. David switched off his flashlight and sat on the bench to his right. From our vantage point, we were closest to the first base side of the field. The security lights and stars shone just enough to make out all of the landmarks of the diamond. The bases, the pitcher's mound, the opposing team's dugout, and the bullpen where the pitchers warmed up. We still had a lot of ground to cover.

The closer we got to the actual location where Ernie had flopped onto the ground, the more confident I was that we would discover some insightful information. The trouble was if we did find a damning clue, how would I explain to Barney the circumstances behind our discovery? The excuse for our being here needed to materialize, and quickly.

I walked past Fiona and navigated to the far end of the dugout, turned, and scanned the entire area. Benches lined the wall inside the small space with an overhead shelf. Phones were at each end of the dugout for coaches to call the bullpen pitchers with instructions. Three sets of steps led to the field. One at each end, one in the middle.

Remembering the circumstances of the game, Ernie must have used a phone to call the dugout. There was probably no way to figure out which one he used. After hanging up, he eventually used one of the sets of steps to head out to the pitching mound to retrieve the ball from Randy and hand it to the new pitcher. I walked to the other end of the dugout to see the view from that angle.

Justin followed me and whispered, "I wonder if he used these steps to get to the field." He pointed to the set to our right.

I peered out to the field as movement appeared on the second-level concourse. I fell to my hands and knees behind the dugout wall. The rest of the group followed suit. My heart beat so hard, I'm sure it was visible through my shirt.

"David." I gestured for him to crab walk toward me. "Are we clear to go to the mound?" Pointing toward the field, I crouched, peeking my head over the railing.

David raised his head, scanning. "I think so." He stood. "We need to make it quick out there."

Yes we did. Realizing we were following the last steps of Ernie's life felt heavy. Regardless of what everyone thought of him, he didn't deserve to die that way, in full view of the entire stadium.

David bent and sprinted toward the mound, then abruptly stopped at the top. I stood next to him, looking back at the dugout. What could someone have done to Ernie that would cause him to keel over right at this spot? We were perched about a foot higher than the rest of the field. Looking at the seating area, I kept my eyes peeled for any further movement.

David nudged me and we followed his jog to the bullpen located behind the fence in left field. We opened the gate and entered the rectangular space. Two mounds the same height as the one on the field were to my right. There was just enough space in here for two pitchers to warm up and a bench for others to sit near a phone at the end, which connected to the same phone in the dugout.

This location was fairly secluded from any view of the wandering guard. Catching my breath, I wasn't sure we were any closer to having answers after all of this risk. Holding my hand up to my ear to detect any approaching footsteps, I felt safe for the minute.

"David, how are we going to get out of here?" There didn't appear to be any escape from the bullpen, and we were in the entirely oppo-site position from where we had entered the stadium, if my sense of direction was correct.

He pointed to a wall behind the pitching mound. Flush with the wall was an embedded door handle. The cadence of footsteps sounded overhead. Instinctively we all ducked as if that would prevent detection. My hand flew to my mouth, and I chuckled at the sight. If we got out of here without being noticed it would be a miracle. As the sound of the footfalls subsided, David led us to the door.

Before opening it, he instructed, "We'll turn right and work our way back to near where we entered. That should get us close to our car."

Nodding, we filed out of the bullpen. David illuminated our path again with his flashlight as we navigated the hallway to the first level of the concourse. I looked around, and my hopes soared that we would get out of here without having to use my contrived excuse to the guard for why we were here. And why we hadn't just gone to the guard's office in the first place. I had no clue if David required medication for any treatments, but that was my phony reason we could try on the guard if needed. It could work.

I saw the exit sign in front of us that would lead to Fiona's car. Just feet away from freedom. But I wasn't sure if we were any closer to nailing the murderer. We would need a debrief from this to share notes since we kept our talking to a minimum inside.

David slowly pushed the crash bar of the door to open it. I balled my fists, hoping an alarm didn't sound and give us up at the eleventh hour. I released my breath as we scurried through, David carefully allowing the door to close as quietly as possible. We did it. At least if we were spotted now nobody could arrest us for trespassing. Beginning as a fast walk and transforming into a sprint we beelined for Fiona's VW bug.

Gasping and wheezing, the giggles started with Fiona and worked their way around the group. "That was awesome," she said.

David reached in and gave her a big hug. What was that about? The two of them definitely had a spark.

Fiona unlocked the doors and we piled inside. As she pulled away, I gazed at the stadium, wondering if my theory was spot on or too crazy to be true.

CHAPTER TEN

Thankfully Linda and I had our baking production down to an assembly line. This morning, all of the energy I had could only take me through the motions. My brain had no power to think about what I was doing. Linda had lined up all of the ingredients in the properly measured amounts to my left for our batches of cupcakes. One by one I dumped them into the super-powered mixer and blended each, the sound of the machine lulling my mind.

Stopping the mixer and lifting the arm, I handed Linda the bowl of batter to pour into the cupcake baking pans. She poured a small amount into each cup, and I retrieved the trays, placing them in the preheated ovens, setting the timer.

"Tilly, you seem extra distracted. Are you OK?" Linda asked, sending the bowls to the sink for washing. She grabbed the spraying arm and gave them a good rinse before placing them in the dishwasher.

"I guess. We were out late last night," I said, not sure how much I should reveal.

Feeling a bit guilty about trespassing, I wasn't convinced it was the right thing to do, basically breaking into the stadium. Sure, I had an excuse at the ready, but still, it didn't sit right with me. And, although I got to see more of the location, my brain couldn't put any more pieces of the puzzle into place. If the players and coaches who chewed gum all had their pouches on the shelf above the bench in the dugout, could it have been an accident that Ernie's got switched with one he was allergic to? It was a routine they had down pat, so what would be different this time? And, with so many people around, how could someone make the switch and not get caught?

I retrieved another bowl for the mixer and moved the ingredients Linda had prepped for the cream filling to my side, dumping them in and starting my mixing again. The rhythmic nature of the process gave me comfort as I further pondered the murder. Not much time remained before the team would resume their games and leave town for the next destination. Would we have any answers before then?

"Hey, you two," came a booming voice from the kitchen door.

Jumping about a foot, my arm inadvertently hit the power switch for the mixer, turning it off. "Uncle Jack. You have to stop doing that!" I admonished.

He proceeded to the sink where Linda continued cleaning up the batter mess as he pecked her on the cheek, the biggest grin plastered on his face. I wasn't sure what put the pep in his step this morning, scaring the bedeedles out of me or seeing his fiancé.

"You're an early bird today," I said, moving over to give him a quick hug.

"Couldn't miss an opportunity to see my two favorite girls," he said.

Linda handed him an apron and a scrub brush, pointing to the sink and giggling. "You can't be back here and not pitch in during our baking time," she said, her warm brown eyes practically glowing.

I couldn't wait for the wedding. They had yet to set a date or plan any details, for that matter. Whatever they decided to do, it would be magical. How could it not be?

"Yes, ma'am," Unkie said and saluted Linda. "Anything for the both of you." He smooched her again on the cheek and took the dishrag from her, taking over the washing.

Glancing at the wall clock, I calculated that Uncle Jack had about an hour before his Checkered Past Antiques opened up. With running his store and Linda working long hours at the bakery, they hadn't had much time together since we had returned from our trip on the Coast Excursion train. Business was doing so well for me that I had hired Dexter. But now I was convinced I needed to recruit more before Linda and I burned out.

I finished mixing the cream filling that would go in the batch of cupcakes when they came out of the oven, scraping the sides of the bowl and setting it aside.

"Tilly," Unkie said over his shoulder to me, "you look tired."

Dang, I couldn't get anything past that guy. I stepped to his side, grabbing a dripping bowl from his hand, and rinsed it off, placing it in the dish drying rack.

"Well, it is early. Justin, Fiona, David, and I were out last night," I said, doubting that brief recap would satisfy his curiosity. He knew better that I wouldn't let Ernie's murder rest until I had answers, especially for David.

"How's David doing?" he asked as he handed me another sudsy dish for rinsing.

Shrugging, I said, "I guess OK. He's such a jokester, sometimes it's hard to tell. We had a chance to hang out, just the two of us. That was nice."

If not for Ernie's murder, I wouldn't have had this special time with my brother. I was grateful for that but anguished about the cause. After our sleuthing at the stadium, my three cohorts and I really hadn't had a chance to debrief with our thoughts. Maybe tonight I could get a few moments with my little Peanut and hope my kitten snuggles could help me think through the convoluted details. Just thinking about that little fur ball relaxed me. Never having a pet before I couldn't have imagined how much she would become a part of my life.

"Oh, yeah!" Unkie spouted as I again jumped, not as relaxed as I thought.

I whacked him with my towel, asking, "Are you enjoying that?" sure he was getting a kick out of teasing me. And certain he was probably spot on assuming why I was so tired. He knew in time I would spill my guts to him. Since moving to Belle Harbor, he had become one of my best friends and like a surrogate father to me.

Linda was working at the table to our left, beginning to plunge cream into our cupcakes, shaking her head at Uncle Jack's antics. My heart warmed deeply that he had found someone who appreciated him the way she did.

"You both should come meet my new employee later," he said, handing me the final dish to rinse. Turning to face the room, he leaned against the sink, drying his hands on a towel.

I smiled. He looked adorable with the blue and white Luna's Bakery and Cafe logo apron, and the scene with the three of us working the baking production was my happy place. "Do tell," I prompted.

"Carlos is a young man, married, and his wife is about to have a baby. He wanted another job to earn some extra money," Uncle Jack explained.

"That's awesome. Can't wait to meet him," I replied.

"I'm going to be doing an orientation today. Since he's got a day job at the newspaper, he's only available weekends for work. But he has a couple of hours off so I can train him." Uncle Jack retrieved the empty cream filling bowl from Linda, swiping his finger inside and tasting the cream. "Mmm," he muttered, closing his eyes.

"I think we've just had a trial run with our prospective part-time employee." I chuckled. "This just confirms to me how much we could use another set of hands on a regular basis."

Unkie washed the bowl, handing it to me. "Wish I could," he said.

"Can't wait to meet Carlos. I'll try to sneak over later with David too," I said. My plan was to keep David as busy as I could to keep his mind off Ernie, not sure if I was succeeding or not.

CHAPTER ELEVEN

The customers had come at a brisk pace today, stocking up on sweets and lunch boxes for their time on the beach. Not many of them stayed in the lobby to eat, prompting me to consider a remodel at some point to create more outside seating. When you could see the ocean from inside the cafe, the strong pull of the beach didn't invite people to linger long.

The whoosh of the door opening behind me prompted me to turn, prepared to greet and serve a customer. To my surprise, David burst in, beaming with a bigger smile than I had seen since he had arrived in town. He beelined toward me for a big hug.

Glancing at the clock on the wall, I said, "You're early." I spun back to the table I was clearing and cleaning, placing empty coffee cups and cupcake wrappers onto a tray.

"Yep!" he said, reaching in for another hug. "Couldn't wait to come see you."

The cups toppled over on the tray, spilling a few drops of remaining coffee as I juggled them. "Aw, that's nice. I'm glad you're here, but I'm not quite ready," I said, placing the tray on the adjoining table to finish wiping up the remaining crumbs.

David carried the tray to the counter, returning to take a seat nearby. "Coach Charlie called," he started.

Whipping my head toward David, I stared at his expression, concerned his cheerful demeanor was about to disappear. While his smile had dimmed, he appeared content, his shoulders relaxed, his hands clasped in his lap.

Continuing he said, "Game resumes tomorrow. Barney will finish interviews today." That was it. No details.

Not able to let it stand there, I asked, "Did he share any info about what was discovered so far?"

Shaking his head and standing, David shoved his hands in his pocket and headed toward the door, gazing at the ocean. Ugh, I went too far in my quest of nosiness, always needing to know details.

"Nope," he confirmed and pivoted toward me. "But I'm confident we'll know something soon." With head down and feet shuffling, he continued, "I try not to think about it. But there's very likely a murderer on the team."

"David." I approached him, my hand on his forearm. "I don't think Barney would allow the game to go on if he wasn't close to an arrest." I tucked my cleaning towel into my apron pocket and hugged him.

"I know. But a little part of me wonders if the killer isn't done yet." He lifted his head.

This was agonizing, seeing my little brother hurting like this. "I'm so sorry. All I can say is try to focus on the positive when one of those thoughts enters your mind. The game will go on. Also, we're about to head down to Unkie's."

David's grin cracked wide open. "That guy," was all he said.

That guy, indeed. "He's got a new employee he's training today but said to come by anytime," I said, lifting my apron over my head and folding it up for the laundry. Thankfully we had ordered several aprons so that we always had a clean one every day. "We're at a lull and Linda said she could handle things for a bit if we wanted to do a quick visit."

I headed to the back with the tray from the table and my apron to inform Linda we were heading out. No doubt David's spirits would soar after the visit with Uncle Jack. "Be right back," I said as David returned to gaze out the front window.

Grabbing my phone, I jammed it in my pocket and returned to the front. "Next time you visit, we need to get you out on the water. The therapy of the ocean is extraordinary," I said and led us toward the boardwalk.

The after-lunch crowd on the beach were up and playing. Splashing in the water, throwing Frisbees, building sandcastles, flying kites. Just seeing the everyday, normal activities relieved some tension. Thankfully, the location of the cafe was a brief jaunt to Uncle Jack's store. When I first pondered leaving my little kitchen in the corner that he had created for me, one mandatory condition was that it be in close enough proximity to continue frequent visits. Especially now with Linda and Unkie engaged, I wanted to keep them close together.

We turned right from the boardwalk and entered Unkie's store. Instinctively, I glanced toward the space that launched my baking business. He had yet to change it up. Was that for lack of time or sentimental reasons? It would be no small feat to have the appliances, counters, and cabinets removed.

Head bowed with his new employee, pointing at several items on a table, Uncle Jack didn't notice us entering.

Clearing my throat, I raised my hand, greeting the duo.

"Tilly. David," Uncle Jack said, heading our direction, arms outstretched for a group hug. "Right on time." He gestured toward where he had been standing, leading us to meet Carlos. "I'm thrilled to introduce you to Carlos."

We shook hands all around.

"We were just going over some of the items I'm donating to the upcoming charity auction," Uncle Jack said, pointing to a collection on the table. "This is one of my prized possessions. I've had it for a while, and it's time it goes to a new home." He held up a large knife with an ornate handle that looked like something Captain Jack Sparrow might brandish. Gently replacing it, he continued, "Carlos, why don't you go ahead and pack up those things we discussed and create the packing list? I'll show you where the catalog is in a bit so you can write up the descriptions for each item."

Stepping to the side to allow Carlos to work, Unkie leaned in, staring at me, and said, "You and Justin have a late night?" Unkie elbowed David as he teased.

My face reddened, not wanting to spill the beans, so I let him think he was on the right track. "Yeah, we did." Well, it wasn't a lie.

Chuckling, he said, "Thought so. I've been so busy getting ready for this auction, I haven't seen Barney lately. Any word?" he asked, glancing back and forth between David and me.

"Well, I think things are progressing," I started, leaving David off the hook. "Sounds like he's almost finished because the game has been scheduled to resume."

David fidgeted next to me, the subject obviously making him uncomfortable.

Grabbing David's arm, Unkie led us to the back where he had a small table and chairs. The memories of this place and our coffee chats flooded back to me. So many conversations about life and my new business. It seemed eons ago now. Glancing toward my old kitchen I asked, "What are your plans for the kitchen?"

"Not sure yet. Maybe I'll take up baking on the side," he said, holding his stomach as it jiggled from laughter.

"Go right ahead," I said, looking at my phone. "I need to head back and relieve Linda. Apparently we're having an afternoon rush." Pointing at both of them, I asked, "Can I count on you two staying out of trouble?"

Unkie's expression of shock doubled me over in laughter. Shaking my head, I began my return trip to the bakery.

CHAPTER TWELVE

I turned the key to lock the cafe door. One of these days we may have offerings for late afternoon and dinner, but for now our hours were for the early birds, lunch crowd, and afternoon snackers. Usually we sold out by then anyway, ensuring our next day's offerings were fresh. The seagulls squawked behind me, scrounging for crumbs left behind by the beach goers.

"Still can't believe you have your own bakery and live here," David said as we headed toward the Ferris wheel.

I planned to squeeze in every second I could while he was in town. He insisted we make our way to Fiona's for a nightcap, which I was all too happy to accommodate. I couldn't see in a million years how a relationship between those two could work out, but you just never knew.

The evening had turned just cool enough to be comfortable without sweating from mid-day heat. The boardwalk was lined with tiki torches, one of my favorite amenities about this town. Though I lived here, the sensation of being on vacation everyday never left. Maybe that was the feeling you got when you were doing what you loved, surrounded by people who had no drama.

"What I meant was, you were so ensconced back in Boston. Back in your former life," David said.

"Yeah, I have to regularly pinch myself too," I replied, navigating us toward the cotton candy stand. "I was scared to death about leaving what I knew. At least I understood those rules and how to operate within them. But I was miserable."

David reached for his wallet, handing the attendant a twenty-dollar bill. "Keep the change," he said as we each took our cones with the light blue swirled sugar. May not be much sleep tonight after the insulin spike from this.

"I knew that. I'm sorry I didn't help out more. I was just so wrapped up in my own world," he said, shoving a handful of the candy into his mouth.

"I'm a big girl. And frankly, I'm grateful for that time and the fact it has led to this," I said, sweeping my arm around. "I've gained so much more confidence to choose those things I want in my life and on my terms."

We strolled quietly for several minutes, finishing our sticky treats. Nearing the Ferris wheel, I spotted Unkie ahead with a few others. Pointing their direction, I guided David. "I think that's Uncle Jack. Let's say hi," I suggested.

Unkie and Linda held hands like they never wanted to let go. The other couple still prompted me to shake my head when I saw them together. Florence, the bookstore owner next door to Checkered Past Antiques, was a tough nut to crack. Granted, we didn't get started on the right foot with her finding a dead body in her store. And it went downhill from there when Justin's and her cat became parents of four adorable kittens, which Fiona, Linda, Unkie, and I had adopted. I wouldn't say she had totally forgiven Justin for his cat's indiscretion, but once the kittens had arrived, it made it a little harder for her to stay mad. And somehow, she and Barney had hit it off and become inseparable, softening Florence even further.

We approached the bench, the four of them appearing very relaxed. For a while after I had arrived in Belle Harbor, I had worried about Unkie's loneliness, although he knew pretty much everyone in town and kept very busy. When fate stepped in and brought Linda, I was over the moon. And turns out, so were they.

"Hey everyone," I greeted. Uncle Jack and Barney stood, a gentle-manly gesture. Laughing, I said, "Sit down, you two." Turning toward Florence, I introduced David. "Florence, this is my brother David."

"Pleased to meet you, ma'am," David said, stepping in front of her, reaching his hand to shake hers, no doubt courting favor with his manners.

"Nice to meet you David," Florence replied, accepting his hand-shake.

"Hey," David started, returning to my side. "If you're not doing anything tomorrow night, why don't you all come to the game? My treat."

The four of them looked at each other, Florence speaking first. "We'd love to. Thank you for inviting us." Barney turned toward her and sat back, appearing surprised at her jumping to accept the opportunity.

"Awesome. I'll leave the tickets at will call. Tilly, let me know where you and Justin have your seats and I'll get four more in that section," David said.

"Sounds good," I replied.

Uncle Jack stood, extending his arm with a bag of saltwater taffy in our direction. "Please help me eat this. I shouldn't have gotten so much, but it's addicting."

David and I looked at each other in unison and busted up.

"What?" Uncle Jack looked around the circle for answers to our reaction.

David grabbed the bag. "OK. I'll take it off your hands. It's just that Tilly and I bought several pounds ourselves. I'll take it to the locker room tomorrow. It'll be gone in no time flat."

Unkie resumed his seat.

Pointing to the wheel, I said, "See you all tomorrow. We need to get to the wheel before it closes for the night"—I thumbed toward David—"and before this guy changes his mind again."

Heading toward the wheel, David dug his hand into the taffy bag, pulling out a purple piece wrapped in wax paper. He turned it over in his hands and put it back in the bag, retrieving a different color. "Tilly, I think we're trying too hard to figure out who killed Ernie. I feel like the answer is right in front of us, but we're trying to force it."

"I'll see if I can worm anything out of Barney, but I agree. I think we have the pieces, but we just need to shuffle them around a bit to re-frame the picture." I stopped and grabbed David's arm. "How bad do you want to go on the wheel?"

He shrugged. "I can take it or leave it. Mostly doing it for you. Why?"

I led us to a vacant bench and sat. Maybe our time was better spent recapping clues. I knew it was difficult for him to talk about this, but until we had answers, the unknown would bother him more. Plopping my backpack on the ground, I retrieved a notepad and pen, holding them in the air. "Aha."

"What are you doing?" he asked, joining me on the bench.

No sense in explaining that I had developed a process to organize clues in previous murders. Knowing that might just prompt him to drag me from this town I loved.

"I love to organize things, as you know," I said, looking at him as he nodded furiously. When he was out at baseball practice while we both still lived at home, I would sneak into his room and arrange his things. He never spoke of it, but I am sure he knew. Sometimes I think he messed them up just to give me something to do.

"Let's get as far as we can. And maybe we can come up with something that can help Barney solve this once and for all." I tapped my notebook with the pen, writing Ernie in the middle and circling his name.

David and I proceeded to fill out the page with everyone who we thought had a motive and would have had the opportunity to do something. Randy and Charlie remained the prominent suspects, but they were now among many others connected to Ernie. Holding the paper out to David, I asked, "Do you think we have anything new?"

Shaking his head, he quietly said, "Nope."

CHAPTER THIRTEEN

Time was ticking on the remaining hours David had left in town. My heart clenched when I thought of him leaving, especially without knowing what happened to Ernie. I shook my head to scatter the negative thoughts, digging into my bucket of popcorn. We had worked through every possibility last night of who could possibly have switched the gum to poison Ernie. Either David wasn't allowing his mind to accept reality of someone he knew being responsible, or we truly hadn't identified the murderer. In any case, this chapter was about to close, perhaps with us never knowing the truth.

I handed the popcorn to Justin before I gulped down the entire bucket ahead of game time. While I would try to enjoy the game, secretly my sole purpose tonight was to see for this one last time if I could unravel the puzzle. Fixated on the field, I noticed the routine was just as David described with warm-ups. The team had emerged first from the locker room, commencing with running and stretching, then tossing the ball back and forth. After about fifteen minutes, the coaches appeared. Charlie started at the plate, hitting fly balls to each of the players in the field. The pitching coaches headed to the bullpen.

Justin held the popcorn out, and I waved it away, obsessed with every detail of activity in front of me. Nothing from the team deviated from the ordinary. "Justin, I don't get it," I said.

"I know," he replied, thankfully munching down on the popcorn to save me from overindulging. "Me either. It just all seems so normal."

Pointing toward the dugout, I said, "The gum bags are lined up behind the bench, same as they were the other day. I'm going nuts trying to figure out what's out of place. It's like those pictures in a magazine where you have to find a specific number of items between the two pictures that are different. I feel like I've got all but the final one."

The announcer came over the loudspeaker to tell us it was about thirty minutes to game time. The grounds crew were smoothing the dirt on the pitcher's mound and laying down the white lines connecting the bases and bordering home plate. Stretching my imagination, I wondered who else in the ballpark we hadn't considered might be possibilities. The announcer? The food vendors? But what would their motive be?

"I'm going to finish this unless you want some," Justin said about the popcorn. "We can get something else before game time, if you want."

"Maybe. Those bonbons were great the other day," I replied.

David raised his hand from the field to catch our attention and jogged our direction as the warm-ups finished. Several players remained on the field and stood in small groups, talking. Passing over the line between third base and home plate, David stumbled and fell. Raising up from his hands and knees, he made a comment to the nearby groundskeeper, earning a dirty look in the process. Standing and brushing grass from his uniform, he resumed his jog our direction.

I stood and gave him a quick hug over the railing in front of me. "Are you OK?"

Turning back toward the field, he said, "Yeah. This isn't the best field in the league. For some reason there seems to be dips in the grass throughout the outfield. One of the guys twisted his ankle last time we played here." Glancing past me, he said, "Unkie not here yet?"

He and the others invited obviously were not. I returned to my seat. "What's going on?" I asked, looking toward the field. "They don't look happy."

"They're not. Charlie is actually switching things up quite a bit from how Ernie ran things," David replied.

"And?" I prompted, wondering what David thought of all of that.

"Well, Ernie was tough, but smart. I think we should have trusted him more and we would have been winning. But sometimes the guys think they know more," David said, glancing back at the field. "The thing is, now they see how Charlie is running the show, they're more appreciative of Ernie and a bit regretful of how they treated him."

"Sorry you have to go through this. Maybe just give it some time. Change is hard," I offered.

Coach Charlie entered the field, holding a hand to each side of his mouth, hollering at the guys. They headed his direction as he gathered them around like he was holding court. Pounding his glove, David said, "Gotta go. Enjoy the game," as he carefully passed by the place he had tripped over and joined the team.

The announcer notified us that he would introduce the players shortly as the game would soon begin. Both teams huddled around their coaches on their respective sides of the field. The grounds crew completed the finishing touches and returned the rakes to the storage location in the corner of the dugouts.

I turned around, shading my eyes to see if I could spot Unkie and the others. I really hoped there hadn't been a mix-up with the tickets.

I pulled out my phone to see if I had a message from him. Nothing. Slowly panning the stands and field, I stopped at each section to evaluate one final time whether there were any suspects I didn't yet have on my list. Either I missed someone or there was a person already there who was escaping detection, somehow a master at blending in to avoid discovery.

The players filed into the dugout, trailed by their coaches, Charlie stopping to shake hands with the head groundskeeper. The umpires emerged from the locker room and gathered around home plate, chatting and checking their notes. I had completely missed considering one of them as a suspect. That would be a logical choice, given strife between coaches and umpires. Wracking my brain for the previous game, I played through each scene, trying to remember if Ernie had any interaction with an umpire. Some coaches were famous for their tempers, even going so far as kicking dirt on the umpire to express their displeasure with the field general's decisions.

Pointing at the officiating crew, I elbowed Justin. "That might be a missing piece," I suggested. "I don't know why it didn't occur to me to look at the umpires."

"Maybe," Justin replied.

If I missed the umpires, who else was I missing? I believed in my gut the murderer was at the game tonight. Only a few hours left before the team wrapped up and headed out to the next town. My excitement grew as my hope soared at the possibility of a breakthrough in the case. I got my notebook out and flipped to a blank page, making a new list. Maybe putting pen to paper would jostle my thoughts with a new way to view the situation. There were four umpires in the officiating crew. I made a line for each of them, in addition to everyone else I had on my list. The home plate and first base umpires were the closest to the visiting team's dugout. With just a few minutes remaining before game time, I slowly scanned the field a final time, scribbling down everyone else that came to mind. I would start with the entire list and remove people by process of elimination according to motive.

CHAPTER FOURTEEN

Hearing rustling behind me, I turned to find Uncle Jack, Linda, Barney, and Florence taking their seats. I had my head buried so deeply in my notes I hadn't heard them. I carefully moved my notebook to the side, trying to keep it from view.

"Tilly?" Uncle Jack said, tipping his head.

Busted. That man didn't miss a thing. "Just making some final notes," I said. Before they had arrived, I had narrowed my list down to just a few people. I couldn't stop now. My brain was on a roll. I turned, my eyebrows raised, inquiring, "Barney?"

"Not quite, kiddo," he replied, digging into the large bucket of popcorn he and Florence were sharing. "Soon, though." What did he know that he wasn't telling me? I studied his expression to see if he was subtly transmitting clues. There was nothing there, other than a desire to spend an enjoyable night with his gal.

Turning toward Florence, I asked, "Have you ever been to a game before?"

Gazing into Barney's eyes, she replied, "No. This is wonderful."

"We might just have a new sports fan on our hands," Barney said, patting Florence's knee.

Everyone from the field lined up on each side to hear the National Anthem. The announcer instructed us to stand as the music began to play. We solemnly faced the flag with our hands over our hearts, singing. I felt my pulse racing, knowing there was no way I could pay attention to the game. The music concluded and we sat, the players taking the field. The umpire threw a ball to the pitcher on the mound, pointing at him, and yelled "play ball."

The first inning was uneventful. A few pop-ups caught, making quick work for both teams. The game was going faster than I had hoped. Leaning in my seat, I looked down at my notebook on the ground to my left, hoping Unkie didn't spot me peeking at it. I had narrowed the suspects down to three. Charlie and Randy had remained on the list as two of the strongest candidates. But the third one newly on the list was also a heavy contender.

The second inning was about to begin, Randy throwing a couple of warm-up pitches to the catcher. The first batter stepped to the plate and cracked the first pitch high over the head of the right fielder into the seats. A home run. Randy turned and kicked the dirt on the mound, pointing at the catcher. Was he blaming him for calling the wrong pitch? Randy shook his arms out, preparing for the second batter, who stepped to the plate. Three pitches to him and Randy was ahead in the count, with two strikes and a foul ball. The fourth pitch followed the identical route as it did for the first batter, flying high into the right upper deck. Uh oh. Was there so much on Randy's mind that he couldn't focus? Was he still upset about Ernie's murder and was there nagging guilt keeping him from concentrating?

The catcher trotted to the mound, his glove covering his mouth as he talked to an animated Randy, flailing his arms. If the catcher couldn't calm him down, it might be an early exit from the game. Randy rolled his head around, stretching his neck as he placed his hand with the ball in his glove, preparing for batter number three. The catcher signaled which pitch to throw, and Randy moved into his windup and rocketed the ball to home plate. Strike one. OK. Maybe it was just jitters after the drama of the last few days. Randy eyeballed the catcher, shaking his head, then standing with the ball in his glove.

He wound up, the ball flying toward the batter and meeting the bat with a crack, flying over the field. Home run number three.

Something had to be bothering Randy. Maybe I could scratch everyone else off my list but him. In his emotional state, perhaps if he was confronted directly with the accusation he might confess. Emerging onto the field, Coach Charlie held his arm out to the umpire, requesting timeout to talk to his pitcher. Randy circled the mound, kicking dirt as Charlie approached. With his hands on his hips, Charlie's head bobbed as he talked. Randy pointed to the catcher again as Charlie shook his head and left the mound, returning to the dugout. Meeting him at the steps from the field, the head groundskeeper handed Charlie a bag of gum. Charlie grabbed it and threw a wad into his mouth, handing the bag back.

Elbowing Justin, I asked, "Did you see that?" as I glanced back at Barney.

"Yeah. Randy got read the riot act. Unless he's perfect from here on out, he's going to be riding the pine," Justin replied.

"No. The groundskeeper. The gum," I sputtered, quickly trying to explain my theory. "Ernie," I continued.

Justin's eyebrows furrowed, not following my line of thinking. Barney continued munching popcorn, not at all dialed in to what was happening. Was it going to be up to me?

"I have to—" I said, speeding down the steps onto the field, toward the dugout. The announcer come over the loudspeaker instructing me to return to my seat or face consequences. I was willing to risk it.

Racing into the dugout, I grabbed the bag of gum the groundskeeper had returned to the shelf and held it out to him. "You poisoned Ernie, didn't you?" I accused, either making the biggest fool of myself for all time or cracking the case wide open.

"Get out of here, lady," the groundskeeper said. "You're nuts."

"Tilly," came David's voice from the field.

I had come this far, there was no going back. "Ernie complained one too many times about your work on the field. You couldn't handle it anymore and decided to do something about it." I replaced the gum on the shelf. "It was easy for you to switch the gum in the bags," I continued.

"Security!" the groundskeeper yelled.

I had my own security. "Barney!" I yelled, waving him to quickly come arrest the guy. Would he believe me?

As the field security approached, I prepared to be taken away. Barney sprinted down the same steps I had taken, on his phone, hurrying toward the dugout, pointing at the groundskeeper.

As if sensing the jig was up, the groundskeeper sped to the other end of the dugout, leaped several stairs, and headed to the bullpen in the outfield. Knowing his escape route from our sleuthing a couple of nights ago, I realized he might have a chance to get away.

"David!" I pointed at the escaping murderer.

David dropped his glove and barreled after him as the groundskeeper's foot found a hole in the grass and he went tumbling. David pounced on him, bringing him to his feet, wrapping him up. Security, followed by Barney, trotted to the outfield, his handcuffs ready.

I bent over, catching my breath. "How did you know?" Charlie asked, staring me down. Little did he know, he was next. The groundskeeper couldn't have pulled this off on his own.

Returning to the dugout, Barney had a second set of cuffs. "Charlie Morrison, you are under arrest for accessory to murder in the death of Ernie Hill."

Charlie looked around, incredulous, sputtering words for how he was being wronged.

"You OK, Tilly?" Barney asked, grinning from ear to ear.

Exiting the dugout, I called to Barney over my shoulder, "I'm great." I headed back to my seat, blowing a kiss to David.

That poor announcer had his hands full keeping the crowd calm in the midst of the on-field antics. This would be a family memory that would last a lifetime.

CHAPTER FIFTEEN

Fiona had set us up with a couple of drinks as we waited for Unkie and Barney to join us. We sat opposite each other in the booth, as I felt a little awkward with what to say. It was obvious that Justin's and my relationship was moving forward. It had been so long since I had been in the dating pool, I didn't know how to act. I clasped my hands in my lap as I sucked some of the drink through the straw. Before this milestone in our relationship, it was easy peasy talking to him. His demeanor was always calm, and he naturally carried a conversation. Now, I felt my brain and mouth were disconnected.

"Tilly, before the others arrive, I have a question for you," Justin said, sitting very still.

Oh boy. I sat back, looking him in the eye, not having a clue where this was going.

"I'd like to take you on a proper date. I know we've been together at some events hanging out, but I want to be sure you're clear how much I like you. And I would like for us to make it official," he said.

Would I ever be ready for this? I leaned slightly forward, my body guiding me to the answer. "I would love that, Justin." My heart fluttered. "Where should we go?"

He sighed deeply, obviously nervous about putting his feelings out there in such a vulnerable way. I hoped I hadn't made him feel uncomfortable. I never wanted to hurt this wonderful man.

"Do you have a preference? I have an idea if you don't," he suggested as he rubbed his hands on his shorts.

"You're more familiar with this town than I am. Are you thinking of something in Belle Harbor?" I asked, pretty much game for anything.

Justin glanced over my shoulder toward the front door and smiled, making me think Barney and Unkie had arrived. "There's a great comedy club the next town over. I thought we could go to dinner and have a few laughs," he said.

I smiled. "That sounds great. We could use some levity after the seriousness of the last several days."

Justin scooted in as Barney and Unkie approached our table. Right behind them, just as they sat, Fiona brought two more drinks that she must have had ready to go.

"Well, that was quite a week. Good to see David again," Uncle Jack said, raising his glass. "To David."

"And to Tilly," Barney said. "Although, what you did, little lady, could have gotten you hurt."

We clinked glasses as I sheepishly bowed my head. He was right. However, nobody was following my line of thinking, and I needed to trust my instincts that were getting more fine-tuned by the day.

"And because I know you're dying to know"—Barney grinned wide and slowly, dramatically sipping his drink before he continued—"both William the head groundskeeper and Charlie will be going away for a long time."

"I get William. Ernie complained one too many times about the field being in poor shape. That field had the most injuries in the league because of how bad it was," I said.

Sports teams tracked an incredible number of statistics about everything, including the playing fields. David and the gang were very familiar with how well the grounds crew maintained each field. I suspect that constant griping wore William down, and Ernie's comments were the last straw.

"It was the obvious motive for Charlie. As the owner's son he expected to be named head coach eventually. But when Ernie was brought in to improve their winning, Charlie began plotting his demise." The server arrived at our table for the order as we sat silently waiting to resume discussion of the case when he left.

"He sang like a canary," Barney continued. "Of course, blaming William for most of it. However, William would never have known about Ernie's allergy if not for Charlie."

The restaurant sounds of happy celebrations, dishes clattering, and music in the background enveloped us. Fiona kept the atmosphere finely tuned to provide both relaxation and joy, both of which she achieved with high marks.

"I'm just glad for David's sake that it didn't turn out to be Randy or any of the players. For a while, it looked like it was headed that direction," I said.

David had called me earlier in the day from the next town where they had a series scheduled to play. The guys were relieved to have answers but still missed Ernie like crazy, realizing his methods would have taken them far. David was so bothered by his discovery in the hat store during our visit that he agonized over finding a possible clue that might implicate his friend. Trust but verify before you share a story you believe to be true. As it turned out, Randy had misplaced his team-issued hat and hadn't had a chance to get a replacement from the team equipment manager, so he bought a cheap knockoff at a souvenir stand near the stadium.

"I really miss seeing that kid," Unkie said. "Maybe we'll have to take another road trip someday to watch him play." Little did he know I was already planning one.

"Well, first, we've got a wedding to plan," I said. "Do you and Linda know yet what you'd like to do?" I was hoping for the winery we visited during our Coast Excursion train trip, but it was entirely their decision.

"Not yet. We've got some ideas."

I punched Unkie. "Let me help you. Or at least I'll be helping Linda," I joked.

"We're pretty busy right now getting ready for the annual charity auction. Thankfully, it's a win-win for me," Uncle Jack said.

The server brought our steaming plates of food. I was so hungry I could have eaten everyone's dish. "What do you mean?" I mumbled as I filled my mouth with the smoked salmon cheddar mac-and-cheese.

"I take the opportunity to donate items that have been in the shop a while. Every year they bring in a lot of money. That way I help out, plus I keep my products fresh," Unkie explained, diving into his burger.

Closing my eyes, I imprinted this scene in my brain, expressing appreciation and gratitude for each and every person at this table. Sitting back, I grabbed my napkin, wiping my face and seeing Justin across from me, mirroring my feeling. Not wanting to get too far ahead of myself for fear of being hurt, I couldn't help but wonder where this was going with him. Could I see myself married and spending the rest of my life with him? *OK, Tilly, reel it in. Comedy club first, then marriage.*

WHAT'S NEXT? SHERBET AND SHENANIGANS

Puppy pals, superstar power, and a vindictive newspaper reporter...

Ninth in the Belle Harbor Cozy Mystery series!

The charity auction to raise money to provide companion dogs for senior citizens is a highlight of Belle Harbor's event calendar. With a collectible knife donated from her uncle's antique shop expected to receive top dollar, Tilly hopes they will set new records.

Before the auctioneer's first call for bids, he is found stabbed to death. The list of suspects is long enough to circle the block. And first in line is Tilly's uncle. With all clues pointing to her uncle, the Belle

Harbor police chief must arrest his best friend for the murder of the auctioneer.

As Tilly races against time to save her uncle, she discovers petty jealousy, long hidden town secrets, and an anonymous donor that cracks the case wide open. Will her uncle go down for the crime and put a wrench in his plans to marry the love of his life? Or can Tilly do his bidding and win the day?

Sneak Peek of Sherbet and Shenanigans

This event brought out almost the entire town. "See anything you can't live without?" I asked Justin as we continued along the tables of silent auction items.

Lifting his arm toward the live auction items, he said, "A surfboard over there has my name on it." We migrated in the direction he pointed: an ocean-blue colored board that stood at least a foot taller than Justin.

"No way you're ever getting me on one of those things," I said. "I need something more solid surrounding me."

"Never say never." He chuckled, rubbing his hand on the smooth resin surface.

"Ladies and gentlemen," came the booming auctioneer's voice over the speakers. "You have sixty seconds for round one in the silent auction. Hurry over to get your favorite items before someone else does."

Looking at Justin, I grabbed his hand, pulling him across the room to the Paradise Hills Resort bid sheet. Dang! Someone outbid me. I looked around to see if the item was being stalked by the winning bidder. I certainly would not arm wrestle someone for it. The crowd sped around, following the auctioneer's advice as he juiced up the excitement. Picking up the pen, I wrote my name on the next blank row.

"Time's up! Pens down!" the auctioneer bellowed.

My arms prickled with goosebumps as I thought of another fun adventure for Justin and me. "Congratulations," he said, his eyes practically sparkling.

"Can I get a picture of you two with your winning item?"

I swiveled around to see Robin Sullivan of the Belle Harbor Gazette, poised with her camera in front of her face, ready to capture the moment.

Looking at Justin, I shrugged, picking up the certificate and holding it in front of me, Justin gently leaning in as Robin snapped the picture.

"Thank you," she said, letting the camera settle to her mid-section at the end of the strap, keeping it at the ready to capture other auction moments. She had done a beautiful piece on Uncle Jack and Linda's engagement, telling a lovely story of their backgrounds and how they met.

Grateful for the attention, I was convinced her articles boosted business at the bakery. "You should come by the bakery again. We've always got new things we're trying," I suggested. It never hurt to ask.

Gazing around the room, she replied, "Yeah, sure," distracted by the bustle of activity for the second round of silent auction items about to close. With a dismissive wave, she departed, speeding around the room, sticking her nose over several bid sheets.

"Why don't we take a seat?" Justin suggested, holding up his bid paddle with number twenty-seven, ready to take that surfboard home as his own.

Meeting us mid-room, Uncle Jack beamed, rubbing his hands together. "Our best turnout yet," he said. "If my calculations are correct, I'm hoping we raise enough to place another twenty dogs and continue the care for the fifty already placed." The Dogs for Seniors program had received national attention, not just for providing companions to single elderly people, but for financing the continued care of the dogs after adoption, even transportation to veterinary appointments.

Justin and I sat in metal folding chairs near the front auctioneering podium.

"I need to do one last check to make sure Clint is ready," Unkie said and disappeared from the room.

The clock on the wall had passed the deadline for bidding on items in the second round, but nobody had announced the closure. The volume of chatter from the crowd escalated as I heard sneers complaining of Clint's inability to run a fair competition.

Linda approached from our left, bending so that we could hear. "I wonder what's going on," she said, looking at the confused faces surrounding us. "I better go find Jack." She exited the main community center room.

I only hoped this blip on the radar didn't diminish enthusiasm for bidding to support this noble cause.

"Where's Clint?" someone yelled. Yes, indeed, where was Clint, and where was Unkie? Something wasn't right, and I stood to go find out what it was before the crowd came any more unglued.

A blood-curdling scream emanated from the hallway to our left, from a voice very familiar. Linda.

ABOUT THE AUTHOR

Sue Hollowell is a wife and empty nester with a lot of mom left over. Finding a lot of time on her hands, and as a lover of mystery novels, she began telling the story of a character who appeared in her head.

The Chemical Bond is a book about Meredith Markette, a young woman who reluctantly enters into the field of law enforcement when her police officer father is killed in the line of duty. Her quest is to discover his murderer and in the meantime come to terms with a tragedy of her youth.

Will this book ever see the light of day? Maybe. Sue really likes the story and character. And writing that book taught her a ton about the publishing industry. Through this experience she has discovered a love of writing stories, and especially mysteries. She hopes you enjoy her books as much as she enjoys writing them.

Connect with Sue on Facebook at www.facebook.com/sueh ollowellauthor and sign up for her newsletter to stay in touch with all things cozy!